DEINONYCHUS

PROTOCERATOPS

LAMBEOSAURUS

POLACANTHUS

AMARGASAURUS

CRYOLOPHOSAURUS

SPINOSAURUS

GORGOSAURUS

SUPERSAURUS

QUETZALCOATLUS

JANE YOLEN

How Do Dinosaurs

Eat Their Food?

Illustrated by

MARK TEAGUE

THE BLUE SKY PRESS

An Imprint of Scholastic Inc. · New York

THE BLUE SKY PRESS

SCHOLASTIC, THE BLUE SKY PRESS, and associated logos are

trademarks and/or registered trademarks of Scholastic Inc.

Library of Congress card catalog number: 2004020761

ISBN-13: 978-0-545-02738-0

ISBN-10: 0-545-02738-1

12 11 10 9 8 7 6 5 4 3 2 1   07 08 09 10 11

Printed in Singapore   46

This edition first printing, June 2007

To wee David, who is a splendid dinosaur
J. Y.

For Michael Cavanaugh
M. T.

How does a dinosaur
eat all his food?
Does he burp,
does he belch,
or make noises
quite rude?

CRYOLOPHOSAURUS

Does he pick at his cereal,
throw down
his cup,

hoping to make
someone else
pick it up?

Does he fuss, does he fidget,
or squirm in his chair?

Does he flip his spaghetti
high into the air?

SUPERSAURUS

DOES

A DINOSAUR

GLARE?

How does a dinosaur
eat all his food?
Does he spit
out his broccoli
partially chewed?

SPINOSAURUS

Does he bubble

his milk?

Stick beans

up his nose?

Does he squeeze juicy oranges

with his big toes?

POLACANTHUS

No . . .

He says, "Please"

and "Thank you."
He sits very still.

He eats all before him
with smiles and goodwill.

He tries
every new thing,
at least one
small bite.

He makes
no loud noises—
that isn't polite.

He never drops anything onto the floor. And after he's finished, he asks for some more.

Eat up.

Eat up, little dinosaur.

DEINONYCHUS

PROTOCERATOPS

LAMBEOSAURUS

POLACANTHUS

AMARGASAURUS

GORGOSAURUS

CRYOLOPHOSAURUS

SPINOSAURUS

SUPERSAURUS

QUETZALCOATLUS